THE BURIAL OF THE RATS

Don't miss out!

Click the button below to receive a Short Story novel By SOPHIE KENT FREE. There's no charge and no obligation.

1

https://game-romance.funnel.heyappjam.com

i

If you leave Paris by the route d'Orléans, after crossing the fortifications and turning right, you will find yourself in a somewhat wild and not at all pleasant place. To the right, to the left, in front of you, behind you rise great heaps of rubbish and rubbish that time has finally accumulated.

Paris has a nocturnal life as well as a daytime one, and a passing traveler who returns to his hotel, rue de Rivoli or rue Saint-Honoré, late at night, or who leaves it early in the morning, can guess, approaching Montrouge - if he hasn't already done so -, what are those big carts that look like boilers on wheels that he finds stopped almost everywhere when he passes by?

Each city has its own institutions, created from its own needs. Thus, one of the most notable institutions in Paris is its population of ragpickers. Early in the morning - and Parisian life begins very early - one can see in most of the streets, placed on the sidewalk in front of each courtyard and each alley, and in the interval of two or three houses, as it exists still in certain American cities, and even in certain districts of New York, large wooden boxes where the servants, or the inhabitants, empty the garbage accumulated during the day. Gather round these boxes, then depart, when the work is done, to other fields of labor and other new pastures, miserable, filthy, starving-looking men and women, whose working tools consist of a bag or a coarse basket carried on the shoulder, and a small rake with which they turn over, probe, examine in the greatest detail the garbage cans. Using their rake, they pick up what they find and place it in their basket with the same ease as a Chinese man uses his chopsticks.

Paris is a centralized city, and centralization and classification are closely linked. At first, while centralization is becoming effective, what precedes it is classification. Everything is grouped, by similarity or by analogy, and from this grouping of groups arises a whole or central unity. A multitude of long arms with innumerable tentacles radiate, while in the center rises a gigantic head with a brain that has the power to understand, piercing eyes that can look in all directions, and sensitive ears to listen - and a voracious mouth to swallow.

Other cities are like all birds, beasts and fish with normal appetites and digestive systems. Paris alone is the analogue apotheosis of the octopus. The product of centralization taken to the absurd, the city is a good representation of the octopus; and there is no aspect where this resemblance is more curious than in the similarity with the digestive apparatus.

These intelligent tourists, who, having abandoned all individuality in the hands of MM. Cook or Gaze, "do" Paris in three days, are often intrigued by the fact that a dinner which, in London, would have cost about six shillings, may not exceed three francs in a cafe in the Palais-Royal. Their surprise would no longer be justified if they were willing to consider classification as a theoretical specialty of Parisian life, and adapt to everything surrounding this datum from which the ragpicker has its genesis.

ii

The Paris of 1850 does not resemble the Paris of today, and whoever sees the Paris of Napoleon and Baron Haussmann can hardly realize the existence of the state of things forty-five years ago.

Nevertheless, one can count among the things that have not changed the neighborhoods where the rubbish is collected. Garbage is the same everywhere in the world, at all times, and the family resemblance between piles of garbage is perfect. Thus, the traveler who visits the surroundings of Montrouge can, without difficulty, go back in his imagination to the year 1850.

That year, I made an extended stay in Paris. I was very much in love with a young lady who, although she shared my passion, had so totally yielded to her parents' wishes that she had promised them not to see me or write to me for a while. Year. I, too, had been forced to agree to these terms, with the vague hope of parental approval. During this period of probation, I had promised to stay out of the country and not to write to my beloved until the expiration of the year. Naturally, time weighed heavily on me. There was no one in my own family or in my circle of friends who could give me news of Alice, and no member of her family had, I regret to say, enough magnanimity to tell me. 'Send even the occasional word of comfort regarding her health or well-being. I spent six months wandering through Europe; but as I could find no satisfactory distractions in these travels, I decided to come to Paris, where at least I would not be far from London, in case some good news should call me there before the appointed time. . That "hope deferred makes the heart sick" was never so true as in my case, because, to my perpetual desire to see the face I loved, there was added an anxiety within me that tortured me because that I was afraid that some accident might prevent me from proving to Alice, when the time came, that during all this long probationary period I had been worthy of her confidence and faithful to my love for her.

Like all travellers, I quickly exhausted the most interesting places, and I was obliged, the second month of my stay, to seek distractions where I could.

After various trips to the more well-known suburbs, I began to guess that there was a terra incognita, unknown to tourist guides, located in the social desert between these alluring places. Accordingly, I began to do systematic research, and each day I picked up the thread of my exploration from where I had left off the previous day.

iii

Over time, my explorations led me near Montrouge, and I realized that in these parts was the Ultima Thule (name given by the Ancients to an island located six days by boat from the north of Great Britain, considered as the northern limit of the world, which would have been reached by Pytheas the Massaliote.

It could be Iceland.) of social exploration - a country as little known as that which surrounds the source of the White Nile. And, thus, I decided to invest philosophically the world of the scavengers, its habitat, its life, its means of existence.

The task was repulsive, difficult to accomplish, and offered little hope of adequate reward. Nevertheless, in spite of common sense, my obstinacy prevailing, I undertook my new investigation with greater energy than I could have had in directed research for any purpose of higher interest or merit.

iv

One day, at the end of a beautiful afternoon in the last days of September, I entered the sanctum of holies in the city of garbage.

The place was obviously home to many scavengers, because some sort of arrangement was evident in the way the piles of rubbish were formed near the road.

I passed among these heaps that stood upright like well-aligned sentries, determined to venture further, and to track down the filth to its ultimate location.

As I advanced, I saw behind the heaps of rubbish a few figures passing here and there, evidently watching with interest the arrival of a stranger in such a place. Their neighborhood was like a little Switzerland, and, zigzagging along, I lost sight of the path behind me.

Eventually I entered what appeared to be a small town or community of scavengers. There were a number of shacks or huts, such as may be found in the more remote parts of the Allan marshes, a kind of rudimentary shelter composed of walls of wicker and earth, and covered with coarse thatch made with barn detritus - shelters such as one would not want to enter for anything in the world, and which, even painted, have nothing picturesque unless they are judiciously treated.

In the middle of these huts was one of the strangest DIYs - I can't say dwellings - I have ever seen. An immense and ancient wardrobe, a colossal vestige of some Charles VII or Henry II boudoir, had been converted into a dwelling.

Both doors were open, so that the entire interior was open to public view. In the empty half of the cupboard, there was a living room about four feet by six, where no less than six old soldiers of the 1st Republic had gathered, smoking a pipe around a coal brazier, wearing torn and thread-bare uniforms.

Obviously, they belonged to the category of bad subjects (in French in the text); their glaucous eyes and pendulous jaws clearly testified to a common love for absinthe; and their eyes had that haggard, worn look, full of the drowsy ferocity that drink immediately engenders in its wake.

The other side of the cabinet remained as in the past, with its shelves intact, except that they had all been cut down to half their depth, and on each of these six boards was a bed made of rags and straw. The half-dozen notables who lived in this building looked at me curiously; and when I turned around, after taking a few steps, I saw their heads brought together for a conversation in low voices.

I didn't like the way it all looked at all because the place was very lonely, and the men looked very, very mean. However, I saw no reason to be afraid and continued, penetrating still further into the Sahara. The path was quite tortuous; and, traversing a series of semi-circles as skaters do when executing the so-called Dutch figure, I became quite aware that I was going astray.

When I had advanced a little further, I saw, round the corner of a half-finished garbage heap, seated on a heap of straw, was an old soldier in a threadbare coat.

" Hey ! I tell myself. The 1st Republic is well represented here, with this soldier. »

When I walked past the old man, he didn't even look at me, but he stared at the ground with emphatic insistence. Again I said to myself, "You see the result of a hard life in war. This old man's curiosity is a thing of the past. »

However, when I had taken a few more steps, I suddenly turned around, and saw that his curiosity had not been extinguished because the veteran had lifted his head and was looking at me with an odd expression.

I had the impression that it was one of the six notables of the cupboard. When he saw me looking at him, he dropped his head; and, without thinking of him any longer, I went on my way, glad that there existed a strange similarity between these old soldiers.

A little later, in a similar way, I met another old soldier. He, too, paid no attention to me when I passed.

With the help of time, it was getting late in the afternoon, and I began to think of retracing my steps. So I turned around to go back, but I could see that a number of paths passed between the different piles, and I wasn't sure which one to take. In my perplexity, I wanted to speak to someone to ask my way, but I saw no one. I decided to continue a few steps further and tried to see if someone could help me - but not a veteran!

V

I reached my goal, because, after about two hundred meters, I saw in front of me a kind of simple hut similar to those which I had already seen, with however for difference that this one was not intended to be inhabited, because it was made simply of a roof and three walls, and it was open in front.

Obviously, everything led me to believe that it was a place where the sorting of garbage took place. Inside the cabin was an old woman, wrinkled and shrunken with age; I approached her to ask her my way.

She got up when I was near her, and I asked her the way. She immediately struck up a conversation, and it occurred to me that here, in the very center of the Kingdom of Garbage, I could pick up details about the history of the rag picker's trade, especially since I could do it from the very mouth of the rag picker. a person who seemed to be the oldest inhabitant.

I began my investigation, and the old woman gave me some very interesting answers - she had been one of the ceteuses (in French) who had sat every day in front of the guillotine, and who had had an active role among the women who had distinguished themselves by their violence during the Revolution. During our conversation, she suddenly says:

- But M'sieur (in French) must be tired of standing?

And she dusted off a rickety old stool so I could sit down. This idea did not appeal to me very much for several reasons; but the poor old woman was so civil that I didn't want to risk hurting her by refusing, and, moreover, the conversation of a person who had been present at the storming of the Bastille might be interesting. So I sat down and our conversation continued.

As we were talking an old man, older and even shrunken and more wrinkled than the woman, appeared from behind the hut. "Here is Pierre," she said. M'sieur can hear stories now, if he wants to, because Pierre was everywhere, from the Bastille to Waterloo. The old man took another stool at my request, and we plunged into an ocean of memories of the Revolution.

vi

This old man, although dressed as a scarecrow, looked like any of the other six veterans.

At that moment I was sitting in the center of the low-ceilinged cabin, with the old woman on my left and the man on my right; the two of them were seated a step in front of me, the room was filled with all sorts of curious wooden objects and many things that I wished I had been away from.

In one corner stood a heap of rags that seemed to want to be abandoned by the abundant vermin that were there, and in another a heap of bones whose smell was somewhat repulsive. Every now and then, glancing at these heaps, I could see the gleaming eyes of some of the rats that infested the place.

All of this was unpleasant enough, but what seemed even worse to me was an old butcher's ax, with an iron handle covered in bloodstains, leaning against the wall to the right. All this did not worry me too much, however. The conversation of the two old guys was so fascinating that I stayed with them as night fell and the heaps of garbage cast deep shadows in the spaces between them.

After a while, I started to feel uneasy. I couldn't figure out how or why, but regardless, I didn't feel at peace. Discomfort is instinctive and has warning value. The psychic faculties are often the sentinels of the intellect, and when they sound the alarm, reason begins to act, although perhaps not consciously.

This is what happened to me. I began to think about where I was and what was around me, and to wonder how I could survive in case I was attacked; and then the thought suddenly came to my mind, although without any obvious cause, that I was in danger.

Prudence whispered to me: "Keep quiet and make no move." So I kept quiet and made no move because I knew four sly eyes were looking at me. "Four eyes, if not more.

My God, what a horrible thought! The hut could be surrounded on three sides by ruffians. I could be the center of a horde of desperadoes such as only half a century of periodic revolutions can produce.

With the sense of danger, my intellect and powers of observation sharpened, and I became more attentive than usual. I noticed that the old woman's eyes constantly turned to my hands. I looked at them in turn and saw the cause of his gaze: my rings. On my left little finger I wore a heavy signet ring, and on my right a valuable diamond.

I thought that, if there was any danger, my first concern must be to remove all suspicion. So I began to direct the conversation to the scavengers' milieu - to the sewers and the things found there; and so, little by little, towards jewellery.

Then, seizing a favorable opportunity, I asked the old woman if she had knowledge of such things. She replied that she had a little. I stretched out my right hand and, showing her the diamond, asked her what she thought of it. She replied that her eyes were bad and leaned over my hand. I say, as nonchalantly as I could:

- Excuse me ! You'll see better that way!

And, removing the diamond, I handed it to her. A light that had nothing of a halo radiated from her withered old woman's face when she touched the stone. She glanced at me as quick and piercing as lightning.

She leaned over the ring for a moment, her face completely hidden, as if examining it. The old man looked straight ahead, in the direction of the entrance to the hut, and at the same time, reaching into his pockets, he took out a cone of tobacco in paper and a pipe which he began to stuff.

I took the opportunity of this momentary pause and respite, feeling unwatched, to look more carefully at the room around me, which was now dark and shadowy in the twilight.

There were always the stinky, messy heaps; the terrible ax, stained with blood, leaned against the wall in the right corner, and everywhere, despite the darkness, the calamitous twinkling of the rats' eyes.

I could even see them through some of the gaps in the boards down below. behind, at ground level. But wait ! Those eyes seemed bigger and brighter and more calamitous than those inside!

vii

For a moment my heart stopped; and I felt my mind seething, a state that makes you feel a kind of spiritual intoxication, as if the body is only standing because it has no time to fall before it pulls itself together. Then, in a second, I was calm, coldly calm, all my energy bound; I was in perfect control, all my senses and instincts on alert.

Now I knew perfectly well the existence of the danger that threatened me: I was watched and surrounded by desperate people! I couldn't even guess how many there were, sprawled on the ground behind the cabin, waiting for the moment to strike. I knew I was big and strong, and they knew it too.

They also knew, like me, that I was English and that, as such, I would defend myself; and so we waited. I had, I felt, taken the advantage for a few seconds, because I was aware of the danger and I understood the situation. Now I thought my courage and endurance were going to be tested. The showdown could come later.

The old woman raised her head and said to me as if she were happy:

- It's really a beautiful ring, a beautiful ring! My God, you know, I used to own such rings, lots of them, and bracelets and earrings! Oh, on those sunny days, I was leading the dance in the city! But they've forgotten me now! They forgot me! "They? They've never heard of me. Maybe their grandfathers remember me, or at least some of them!

And she gave a discordant, croaking laugh. I must say that then she surprised me, because she handed me the ring with a sort of grace which recalled the manners of the past and which was not lacking in pathos.

The old man stared at her with an air of sudden ferocity, then, half rising from his stool, suddenly said to me in a hoarse voice:

- Let me look!

I was about to hand the ring when the old woman said to me:

- No ! No ! Don't give it to Peter! He's a crazy old man! He loses everything! Such a pretty ring!

- Viper! said the old man wildly.

Then the old woman exclaimed, louder than necessary:

- Wait! I'm going to tell you something about a ring.

There was something in the tone of her voice that worried me. Maybe it was because I was too impressionable, pissed that I was at this point of excitement, but I thought I guessed she wasn't talking to me. As I looked around the room, I saw the eyes of the rats in the piles of bones, but I no longer saw the eyes of the men behind in the cracks of the hut. But even as I looked around for them, I saw them appear again. The "Wait! of the old woman gave me respite to attack, and the men lay down again in the same posture.

viii

Once I lost a ring, a beautiful diamond ring that belonged to a queen and was given to me by a farmer general who later cut his own throat because I refused his advances; I thought it had been stolen and blamed it on my servants, but found no trace of it.

The police came and suggested the ring ended up in the sewer. We went down - me in my beautiful clothes - because I couldn't trust them when it came to my beautiful ring. I know the sewers better since that time, and the rats better too!

But I will never forget the horror of this place, teeming with shining eyes, a wall of eyes before the light of our torches! And finally, we arrived under my house. We searched and surprisingly found my ring!

But we also found something else before going out! As we reached the opening, a group of sewer rats - human rats this time - approached us. They told the police that one of their own went down the sewer but did not come out. He had entered only a short time before us and had gotten lost, he couldn't have been very far. They asked for our assistance in finding him, and so we left. They tried to prevent me from accompanying them, but I insisted. It was a new adventure, and hadn't I found my ring? We didn't get far before we hit on something.

There was little water, and the bottom of the sewer was raised with bricks, garbage and the like. They' was beaten, even when his torch had gone out. But they were too many for him! It didn't take them long! The bones were still warm, but cleaned!

They had even eaten their own dead, and there were rat bones as well as human bones. They took it pretty calmly, the others - the human bones - and they joked about their comrade after they found him dead, though they would have helped him if they found him alive. Bah! No matter life or death!

- And you weren't scared? I asked her.

- Fear? She said laughing. Me, be afraid? Ask Peter. It's true that I was younger then, and when I walked through that horrible sewer, with its wall of hungry eyes, still moving around in the circle of torchlight, I didn't feel like... comfortable.

But I continued to advance in front of the men, that is how I do. I never allow men to get ahead of me. All I ask is to have an opportunity and the means! And they ate it - they erased every trace, except the bones; and no one knew, and no one had any news of him!

ix

At that moment, she gave a fit of giggles, the most macabre gaiety that I have ever had the opportunity to hear and see. A great poetess describes her heroine who sings: "Oh! to see or hear her sing! I hardly know which of the two is more divine! »

This same idea could have been applied to the old woman - anything but the divine, because I could hardly have said which of the two was more infernal, or her laughter, hard, malevolent, satisfied and cruel, or the sneer and the sneer. the horrible, decayed opening of her mouth like a tragic mask, and the yellow glow of a few discolored teeth in the shapeless gums.

With that laugh and with that sneer, and the chuckling satisfaction, I knew as well as if someone had spoken to me in thundering words that my murder was sealed and that the murderers were only waiting for the favorable moment for its accomplishment. .

I could read, between the lines of her dismal story, the orders to her accomplices. "Wait," she seemed to say, "Wait, I'll strike first." Find me the gun and I'll grab the occasion. He won't escape. Keep it quiet and no one will know anything. There will be no screaming, and the rats will do their job. »

It was getting darker and darker, night was coming. I peeked inside the cabin; nothing had changed! The bloody ax in the corner, the piles of trash and the eyes on the piles of bones and in the cracks near the floor.

Pierre was still ostensibly busy filling his pipe, then he struck a match and began to draw on the pipe. The old woman says:

- My dear heart, how dark it is! Peter, be a good enough boy and light the lamp.

Pierre got up and, with the lighted match in his hand, touched the wick of the lamp which hung on one side of the entrance to the cabin, and which with its reflector threw light into the room. It was obviously used at night for sorting garbage.

- Not that, idiot! Lantern! She cried.

He immediately extinguished the lamp, saying, "All right, Mom, I'll find it," and he quickly went to the left corner of the room. The old woman said in the dark:

- Lantern! Lantern! Oh! It is the light which is most useful to us poor people. The lantern was the friend of the Revolution! She is the rag pick-er's friend. It helps us when all else fails us.

She had scarcely said these words when a kind of creaking was heard throughout the cabin and something was pulled smoothly onto the roof.

Again, I could half-understand. I knew the lesson of the lantern:

- Let one of you climb on the roof, with a knot, and move away when he comes out, if we fail inside.

As I peered through the opening, I saw the knot in the rope looming black against the colored sky. Now I was trapped!

X

Pierre was not long in finding the lantern. I kept my eyes fixed in the darkness on the old woman. Pierre struck a match, and I saw the old woman take from the ground, beside her, where it had mysteriously appeared - it was hidden in the folds of her skirt - a long, sharp knife. It looked like a butcher's sharpening iron with a sharp point.

The lantern was on.

- Bring it here, she said. Put it in front of the door where we can see it. Look how beautiful she is! She holds back the darkness. That's exactly what it takes!

Exactly what was needed for her and her purposes. The lantern threw all its light on my face, leaving in shadow the faces of Pierre and the woman, both of whom were quite a distance on either side.

I sensed that the time to act was approaching, but I knew now that the first sign and the first movement would come from the woman. So I looked at her.

I wasn't armed at all, but I had decided what to do. On the first move, I'd grab the butcher's ax in the right-hand corner and work my way out. At least I would die bravely. I took a quick look to determine the exact position of the weapon in order to be able to grab it on the first try, now or never time and precision were precious.

Good God, she was gone! All the horror of the situation reflects on me. But the bitterest thought of all was that if the outcome of this terrible situation were to turn against me, Alice was bound to suffer. Either she would think me unfaithful - and any lover, or anyone who has ever been in that position, can imagine the bitterness of that thought - or she would continue to love me long after I was lost to her and the world, so that her life would be broken and filled with bitterness, and torn to pieces by disappointment and despair. The very extent of my pain strengthened me and enabled me once again to bear the appalling gaze of these plotters who stared at me.

I don't think I betray myself. The old woman looked at me as a cat looks at a mouse: her right hand was hidden in the folds of her skirt, clutching, I knew, her long, sinister-looking knife. If she had seen any fear appear on my face, she would have, I felt, realized that the time had come and would have jumped on me, like a tigress, sure to surprise me defenseless.

I looked out into the night, and there I saw a new cause of danger. In front of and around the hut, at a short distance, black shadows were profiled; they were certainly still, but I knew that they were all alert and on their guard. There was little chance for me now to escape in that direction.

Again, I looked around the cabin. In times of strong emotion, and of great danger which provokes emotion, the mind works very rapidly, and the acuity of the faculties depending on the mind increases in proportion. This is what happened at this time. In an instant I understood the whole situation. I realized that the small ax had been taken out through a hole made in one of the rotten planks, and how badly this one was so that such a thing could be done without the slightest noise.

The hut was a regular kill-trap, and was guarded on all sides. A man, tourniquet in hand, was lying on the roof, ready to take me into his noose if I managed to escape the old witch's knife.

Ahead of me, the path was guarded by I didn't know how many sentries. And behind the hut waited a row of desperate men. I had seen their eyes again through the gap in the planks at ground level when I took one last look, as they lay waiting for the signal to spring to their feet. If I ever had to do something, now was the time!

xi

As nonchalantly as I could, I pivoted slightly on my stool to get my right leg well under me. Then, with a sudden leap, turning my head while protecting it with my hands, and moved by the energy of the knights of the middle Ages, I pronounced the name of my lady and threw myself against the back wall of the hut.

As vigilant as they were, the suddenness of my gesture surprised Pierre as much as the old woman. As I smashed the rotting planks, I saw the bewildered old woman jump up like a tigress, and heard her weak gasp of rage.

My feet landed on something that moved, and as I jumped forward I knew I had put my feet on the back of one of those prone men outside the shack.

I was scratched with nails and splinters of wood, but I was not hurt. Out of breath, I climbed the mound in front of me, hearing, as I ascended, the dull fall of the cabin as it crumbled like a mass.

The ascent was a nightmare. The heap, though low, was terribly steep, and with every step I took the mass of rubbish and ashes descended with me and gave way under my feet. The dust rose and choked me, it was nauseating, fetid, dreadful; but my ascent was, I felt, a matter of life and death, and I plodded along.

The seconds seemed like hours to me; but the few seconds ahead at the start, combined with my strength and my youth, gave me a great advantage, and as several figures advanced behind me, in a deep silence more menacing than any sound, I arrived without difficulty at the top of the mound.

The mound was one of the highest in this region of filth, and as I climbed to the top, gasping for breath, my heart beating like a great hammer, I saw in the distance to my left the full red glow of the sky, and closer the twinkling of lights. Thank God! I now knew where I was and where the road to Paris passed!

xii

For two or three seconds, I paused and looked behind me. My pursuers were still well behind, but climbing resolutely and in dead silence. Beyond, the cabin was a ruin, a mass of planks and moving shapes. I could see it easily because flames were already coming out of it. The rags and straw had evidently caught fire in the flame of the lantern. Silence, again! Not a sound! Those poor old folks could at least die properly!

I only had time to take a quick look, because as I looked around me to prepare to descend, I saw several dark shapes gathering on either side to bar my arm. Now it was a life and death race. They were trying to stop me from taking the road to Paris, and so, instinctively, I quickly descended on the right side. I arrived just in time, because, although it seemed to me to descend the slope in a few steps, the cunning old men who were watching me turned back, and one of them, at the moment when I slipped into the open space between two heaps in front of me, almost succeeded in hitting me with a blow of the terrible butcher's axe. Surely he does.

Then began a truly horrible hunt. I easily outstripped the old men, and even when a few younger men and several women joined in the chase, I easily outdistanced them. But I didn't know the way, and I couldn't even guide myself by the light in the sky because I was running the other way. I had heard that unless there was a reason to do otherwise, men who are pursued always turn left, and so I did; and I think my pursuers knew it also, they who were more animals than men, and who, either by cunning or instinct, had discovered such secrets for their use.

So that, finishing my quick run, after which I intended to catch my breath, suddenly, I was really, now, in the spider's web! But the thought of this new danger aroused in me the resource of the pursued beast, so that I descended by taking the nearest path on the right.

I continued in that direction for a hundred yards, and then, turning left again, realized that I had doubtless avoided the danger of being surrounded.

But not that of the pursuit, because the rabble came towards me, tidy, determined, implacable, and always in a threatening silence.

In the deeper darkness the heaps now seemed to be smaller than before, though - because night was coming - they seemed larger in proportion. I was now well ahead of my pursuers, and quickly climbed the heap in front of me.

O happiness of happiness! I was almost on the edge of this garbage hell. Far behind me, the red light of Paris lit up the sky, and rose behind the heights of Montmartre a dim light, with here and there points shining like stars.

My strength regained after a while, I jumped running over the remaining heaps, smaller and smaller in size, and found myself further on on flat ground. The prospect, however, was not reassuring. Everything before me was dark and gloomy, and I had evidently come upon one of those marshy wastelands in the hollow of a depression, which are found here and there near large cities.

Desolate places, covered with rubbish, whose space makes it possible to store as a last resort all that is harmful - the land is so poor that no squatter, even the most miserable, wants to occupy it .

Eyes accustomed to the darkness of the night, and far now from the shadow of those awful heaps of garbage, I could see much better than before. Perhaps the reason for this was that the reflections in the sky of the lights of Paris, although the city was a few kilometers away, were also reflected here. Anyway, I could see well enough to find my bearings, at least at some distance around me.

Ahead of me was a desolate piece of land that seemed absolutely flat, with the scattered shadowy reflections of stagnant ponds. Apparently, far to the right, among a small group of scattered lights, loomed the dark mass of Fort Montrouge, and to the left, farther off, dotted by the scattered rays from the windows of the pavilions, the lights in the sky indicated the locality of Bicetre. After thinking for a moment, I decided to turn right to try to reach Montrouge. There, at least, I would enjoy relative safety, and it was possible that I might come across some of the crossroads I knew well beforehand. Somewhere, not far away, must have been the strategic road, built to connect the outer chain of forts that encircle the city.

Then I looked behind me. Crossing the heaps of garbage, emerging in black against the light of the horizon, several silhouettes moved, and I saw, a little more on the right, several others deploying between me and my destination. It was obvious that they wanted to block my path in this direction, and so my choice became limited: I had to either continue straight or continue left. Leaning down to fix my sights on the horizon, I looked carefully in that direction, but I could not detect any presence of my enemies. I figured that since they weren't defending or trying to defend that position, it was obviously dangerous for me to go there. So I decided to continue straight ahead.

xiii

It was not a happy prospect, and as I progressed the reality grew worse. The ground had become soft and spongy, and from time to time gave way under my feet, making me a little sick.

I had more or less the feeling of going down, because I saw around me parts of the ground higher than the one on which I was, and this in a space which, at some distance, seemed absolutely flat.

I looked around, but couldn't see any of my pursuers. It was strange because every moment those night owls had followed me in the dark as easily as if it were broad daylight. How I blamed myself for going out dressed in my light-colored tweed tourist suit!

The silence and my inability to pierce my enemies, as I felt them staring at me, getting horrid, and in the hope that someone who wasn't part of this horrible team could hear me, I began to scream, raising my voice, several times.

Not the slightest answer; not even the echo of my voice rewarded my efforts. For a moment, I remained quite inert, and fixed my gaze in front of me. On one of the raised parts of the ground around me, I saw a dark shape moving, then another, and yet another. This to my left, and apparently to cut me off.

I thought that again I could, thanks to my ability to run, get out of the game of my enemies, so, at full speed, I rushed.

Fuck!

My feet gave way on a mass of slimy garbage and I fell full length into a stinking, stagnant pond. The water and mud in which my arms sank to the elbows were filthy and foul beyond description, and in my sudden fall I even swallowed a little of this disgusting substance which nearly suffocated me and made me gasp to catch my breath.

I will never forget those minutes I lay there, trying to recuperate, almost forgetting the fetid smell of that dirty pond from which rose a ghostly white mist. Worst of all, besides my increased despair as a hunted animal which sees the pack of hunters closing in on him, was to see in front of me, while I remained helpless,

It is a strange thing the way our mind works on various subjects, even when our thought employs all its energy in concentrating on a terrible and pressing necessity.

I was, at this very moment, in a situation that put my life in danger, my salvation depended on what I was going to do, the need to choose was becoming more and more pressing, and yet I could not help to think of the strange and relentless persistence with which these old men pursued me.

Their silent resolve, their constant and ruthless stubbornness, even for such a cause, elicited as much as fear an ounce of respect. What vigor they must have had in their youth!

Now I could understand the swirling charge of the Arcole bridge, the contemptuous exclamation of the old guard at Waterloo! Unconscious celebration has its own pleasures even at such times: but fortunately it is not at all incompatible with the thought from which the action arises.

I understood at a glance that, until now, I had failed in my enterprise; my enemies, for the moment, had won. They had succeeded in surrounding me on three sides, and they were determined to deviate me to the left, where the danger reigned, since they had left no sentries. I accepted the alternative - it was the case of the choice of Hobson -, and I rushed. I had to stay on the lower part of the site since my pursuers occupied the higher part.

Nevertheless, although the spongy ground and uneven ground delayed me, my youth and my training enabled me to keep the distance, and, by following a diagonal line, I not only prevented them from approaching, but also began to remove.

This gave me courage and new strength, and in such a moment the effect of my regular training began to be felt and I found my second wind. In front of me, the ground rose slightly.

I quickly climbed the slope and found a stretch of silty water, and beyond that a dyke or bank that looked black and eerie. I felt that if I could reach the dike, there I could, safely, with solid ground under my feet and some semblance of a path to guide me, find a comparatively easy way to escape my enemies.

After glancing right and left, and seeing no one in my immediate vicinity, I focused my attention for a few minutes on watching where I would step as I walked through the swamp. It was a difficult and strenuous crossing, but one that did not present any danger and only required some effort.

Shortly after I reached the dyke. I climbed the slope exulting; but there again, I received a new shock. On either side of me rose several crouching figures. Coming from right and left, they threw themselves on me. Each held a rope in one hand.

I was almost completely surrounded. I couldn't pass either way, and the end was near.

There was only one chance, I took it. I threw myself across the dyke and, escaping the clutches of my enemies, jumped into the river.

At any other time I would have found this water to be infested and filthy, but now it was as welcome as the pure river to the thirsty traveler! She was the road by which I could save myself!

My pursuers rushed after me. If only one of them had held the rope, it would have been my end, because he could have tripped me with it before I had time to do a breaststroke. But as they were all holding it, they were embarrassed and so they fell behind, and when the rope hit the water, I heard the "floc" far behind me. In a few minutes of energetic breaststroke, I crossed the river, refreshed by the immersion and encouraged by my dodging. I climbed the dike, the mood relatively cheerful.

From above, I looked behind me. Through the darkness I saw my assailants scatter back and forth along the sea wall. Obviously the chase was not over, and again I had to choose a direction. Beyond the dyke where I was, stretched a wild and marshy space, very similar to that which I had crossed. I decided to avoid such a place and considered for a moment whether I would go up or down the dyke. I thought I heard a noise, the muffled noise of an oar, so I listened, then shouted.

No response, but the noise stopped. My enemies had apparently procured a boat or some other craft. Since they were on the upper part of the dike, I took the path down and started running. As I passed to the left of where I had entered the water, I heard several light, furtive "plops," like the sound a rat makes when it dives into the water, but much louder; and as I looked I saw the dark reflections of the water broken by the ripples around several advancing heads. A few of my enemies were also swimming in the river.

And now, behind me, upstream, the silence was broken by the rapid rattling and creaking of oars; my enemies stalked me. I balanced on my best leg and resumed my run. Two or three minutes later I looked back, and by the help of a ray of light which pierced the shapeless clouds, I saw several dark figures climbing the bank behind me. Now the wind had picked up, and the water beside me was choppy and beginning to break into small waves against the shore. I had to keep my eyes pretty much fixed on the ground in front of me, lest I stumble, because I knew that to stumble was death. I turned around a few minutes later. On the dyke were a few dark figures, but crossing the marshy wasteland, there were many more. What new danger should I expect? I didn't know, I could only guess. Then, as I resumed my course, it seemed to me that my path was still descending to the right. I looked upstream, saw that the river was much wider than before, and that the dike I was on was disappearing; beyond it flowed another river, where I saw, on its nearer bank, some of the dark shapes that had now crossed the marsh. I was on some kind of island.

My situation was now really desperate, because my enemies were blocking me from everywhere. Behind me, the sound of the oars became faster, as if my pursuers sensed that the end was near. Around me, on all sides, was desolation; as far as I looked, there was no roof or light. In the distance, on the right, stood some dark masses, but I did not know what they were. I paused for a moment to consider what I should do, not to go any further, but because my pursuers were closing in. I made my decision quickly. I slid down the bank and entered the water. I headed straight ahead to catch the current, getting out of the still water around the island, certain now that I was in the river, that it was indeed an island. I waited for a cloud to pass through the moon and leave everything in darkness. Then I took off my hat and put it gently on the water so that it floated; a second later, I dived to the right, and began to swim underwater with all my might. I spent, I think, half a minute underwater, and when I surfaced, as gently as possible, I turned to look back. A little further on floated gaily my light felt hat. Immediately behind came a rickety old boat, propelled furiously by a pair of oars. The moon was still partly obscured by clouds floating around, but in the imperfect light I could see a man, standing at the bow of the boat, holding air, ready to strike, which seemed to me to be that terrible ax which I had escaped before. As I watched, the boat got closer and closer, and the man kicked wildly. The hat disappeared. The man fell backwards, almost overboard. His comrades held him back, but not the axe, and as I turned and swam with all my might for the farther shore, I heard the curse uttered in a low voice by my baffled pursuers.

xiv

It was the first human word I had heard since the beginning of this dreadful hunt, and although it was full of threats and dangers for me, I felt pleasure, because it broke the terrible silence that surrounded me and terrified me.

It was the tangible sign that my enemies were men and not ghosts, and that at least I could fight as such, although I was alone against many.

But now that the spell of silence was broken, the noises came, deaf and fast. From ship to shore, and from shore to ship, questions and answers were exchanged, swiftly, with fierce whispers.

I looked back, a fatal gesture if ever there was one, because at that moment someone saw my face, the whiteness of which stood out against the dark water, and shouted.

Hands were stretched out in my direction, and almost immediately the boat took off again and rushed off. I had only a short distance to cover, but the boat approached faster and faster behind me. A few more fathoms and I was on shore. But I felt the boat coming, and expected every second to feel the blow of an oar or some other weapon on my head. If I hadn't seen that terrible ax disappear in the water, I don't think I would have reached the shore.

I heard the oaths uttered by the men who were not rowing, and the breathlessness of the rowers. After a supreme effort to save my life or my freedom, I touched the bank and climbed it.

There was not a single second to lose, because immediately behind me the ship was approaching, and several dark shapes were jumping in pursuit. I reached the top of the dyke and, heading to the left, continued to run.

The boat started and followed in the river. I saw what was happening, and fearing danger in that direction, I quickly turned around, descended the dyke on the other side; after passing a small stretch of marsh, I reached a wild, open and flat place,

Always behind me, my pursuers chased me relentlessly. Far ahead, below me, I saw the same dark mass that I had seen before, but it was now getting closer and more imposing. My heart beat wildly because I guessed that it must be Fort Bicêtre, and regaining my courage, I continued on my way.

I had heard that between each of the forts that protect Paris there were strategic routes, deeply dug trenches, where the moving soldiers could take shelter from the enemy. I knew that if I could gain that path I would be safe, but in the darkness I could see no sign of it, so in the blind hope of reaching it I kept on running.

Shortly afterwards I came to the edge of a deep trench, and found a road below me protected on either side by a water-filled ditch, fenced in on either side by a high, straight wall.

Growing weaker and weaker, and my head spinning more and more, I continued to run; the ground became more and more uneven, more and more, until I tripped and fell; I rose again, and continued to run with the blind anguish of a hunted animal.

Again, the thought of Alice made me nervous. I didn't want to disappear and ruin her life like that; I would defend myself and fight until the final test. With great effort, I clung to the top of the wall. As I pulled myself up like a trapeze artist, I clearly felt a hand touching the sole of my shoe. Now I was on a kind of road, and I saw in front of me a light shining dimly. Blinded and dizzy, I kept on running, stumbled and fell,

XV

Halte-là (in French)!

- The words echoed like a celestial voice. A bright light, it seemed to me, surrounded me and I cried out with joy.

- Who goes there (in French)? (The metallic clink of weapons, the glint of steel before my eyes: instinctively I stopped, as, close behind me, my pursuers charged forward.)

A word or two more, and from the wicket came what seemed to me like a tide of red and blue as the guard came out.

Everything around seemed to fill with light, the glint of steel, the clank and clang of weapons, and loud, gruff voices giving orders.

When I fell forward, completely exhausted, a soldier caught up with me. I looked behind me, terrified by the expectation, and saw the group of figures disappearing into the night.

Then I had to faint. When I regained consciousness, I was in the duty room. They gave me a glass of brandy, and soon after I was able to tell them part of what had happened.

Then a police commissioner appeared, seemingly out of nowhere, as a Parisian police officer usually does. He listened carefully, and then deliberated for a moment with the duty officer. They probably agreed, because they asked me if I was ready now to accompany them.

- To go where? I asked as I stood up.

- Back to the garbage heaps. Maybe we'll catch them again!

- I'll try, I say.

He looked at me fixedly for a moment and said abruptly:

- Would you like to wait a bit, or even until tomorrow, my young Englishman?

It touched my heart, like maybe he wanted it, and I jumped to my feet.

- Let's go now, I say, now! now! An Englishman is always ready to do his duty!

The commissary was as good-natured as he was sagacious; he patted me on the shoulder in a friendly way:

- Good boy! he said, forgive me, but I knew what would do you the most good. The guard is ready. Let's go!

So, after crossing the guard room and following a long vaulted passage, we went out into the night. A few of the men in front had powerful lanterns. We crossed the courtyard and descended a sloping path, to emerge under a postern into a sunken path, the same as the one I had seen in my flight.

The soldiers were ordered to march at a gymnastic pace, and with a brisk leaping step, half running, half marching, they advanced rapidly. I felt my strength returning again - such is the difference between a hunter and a hunted.

A very short distance separated us from a pontoon, low in profile, which crossed the river, and apparently very little upstream from the place where I had crossed it. We had probably tried to damage it somewhat, because all the ropes had been cut and one of the chains had been broken. I heard the officer say to the commissioner:

- We're just in time! A few more minutes and they'd destroy the bridge. Forward! Even faster! (And we went on.)

Again we approached a pontoon on the bend of the river; on arriving, we heard the hollow "boom" of metal drums as they sought to destroy this bridge as well. A word of command was issued, and several men aimed their rifles.

- Fire! A salvo rang out. A muffled cry arose, and the dark figures dispersed. But the damage had been done, and we saw the far end of the pontoon swaying in the river. This caused a serious delay, because it took us almost an hour to replace the ropes and restore the bridge to a place strong enough to cross it.)

xvi

We resumed the hunt. We were moving faster and faster towards the piles of garbage. After a while we came to a place I knew. There were the remains of a fire - some still smoldering wood ashes cast a red glow, but most of the fire was cold. I recognized the site of the cabin, and behind the pile I had climbed; in the reddening of the ashes, the eyes of the rats still shone with a kind of phosphorescence. The purser addressed a word to the officer who shouted:

- Stop!

The soldiers were ordered to scatter around and keep watch, then we began to examine the ruins. The commissioner himself began to lift the burnt planks and the charred debris. Soldiers gathered them together by piling them up. Shortly after, the commissary stepped back, leaned over and waved to me as he straightened up:

- Look ! he said.

It was a horrible sight. There was a skeleton lying face down on the ground: a woman, apparently. Between the ribs stood a stake, long as a sword, like a butcher's sharpening knife, the sharp point of which was driven into the spine.

- You will notice, said the commissioner to the officer and to myself, taking out his notebook, that this woman must have fallen on her knife. Rats are swarming here - look at their eyes shining in this pile of bones - and you'll also notice (I shudder when he ran his hand over the skeleton) that they haven't wasted much time. The bones are barely cold!

No other presence appeared in the area, dead or alive; reforming in line, the soldiers resumed their journey. We arrived soon after at the hut built with the old cupboard. We approached it. Old men in five of the six compartments were sleeping - asleep so soundly that even the light of the lanterns did not wake them. They looked decrepit, sinister and gray with their emaciated, wrinkled and weathered faces and their white whiskers. The officer gave them a harsh order in a loud voice, and instantly each of the six old men was standing in front of us, standing to attention.

- What are you doing here?

- We are sleeping, they answered.

- Where are the other scavengers? asked the commissioner.

- Went to work.

- And you?

- We're on call.

- Plague! said the officer, laughing sardonically, looking the old men one after the other straight in the face. (Then he added, with cold and deliberate cruelty:) Asleep at your post! Is this the old guard way? Waterloo, so nothing surprising!

Illuminated by the light of the lantern, I saw the old and grim faces turn pale as death, and I nearly shuddered at the expression in their eyes when the soldiers echoed the officer's ruthless banter.

I felt at that moment that, to some extent, I had my revenge.

For a moment they looked like they were about to throw themselves at the man who was insulting them, but years of soldiering had dragged them down and they remained silent.

- There are only five of you, said the commissary; where is the sixth? (The answer fell with a sinister chuckle.)

- Here it is! (And the speaker pointed to the bottom of the cupboard.) He died last night. You won't find much of it. It's fast, the burial of rats!

The purser leaned over to look inside the cupboard. Then he turned to the officer and said calmly:

- Might as well leave. There is no trace now; nothing proves that this man was the one who was wounded by the bullets of your soldiers! They probably killed him to erase all traces! Look! Again he bent down and put his hands on the skeleton. "The rats work fast and there are plenty of them." The bones are still warm!

I shudder, and many others around me did the same.

- Train yourself! said the officer, and thus lined up in marching order, the lanterns swinging forward, the veterans in handcuffs in the center of the group, we left the heaps of rubbish at a rapid pace to take the Fort de Bicêtre.

My year of probation is long over, and Alice is my wife. But when I look back on that difficult twelve month period, of all the incidents that come to mind, the most vivid is the one associated with my visit to the City of Garbage

End

Don't miss out!

Click the button below and you can sign up to receive emails whenever we publishes a new book. There's no charge and no obligation.

https://game-romance.funnel.heyappjam.com/[1]

Will[2] you love to read "THE MISSING FISHING BOAT ON A FRENCH IS-
LAND?" That is one of our Best Sellers on Amazon. Check it out Below.

https://www.amazon.com/dp/B09X5XD7JN

THEN YOU SHOULD READ OTHER stories in our collection.

https://www.amazon.com/dp/B09X38WT6R

The Time Of A Harvest

https://www.amazon.com/dp/B09X366C78

---

2. https://game-romance.funnel.heyappjam.com/Will